Dedicated to all of the
dreamers out there...

Published by Trism Books, Deerfield, IL, USA

WRESTLING DREAMS

Wrestling Dreams/written by Colt Cabana with Sam Weisz and Erica Weisz; illustrated by Erica Weisz.

ISBN 978-0-9888338-7-6

1. Wrestling - Juvenile Literature 2. Self Esteem - Juvenile Literature 3. Friendship - Juvenile Literature. I.Title.
The artwork was created in ink with watercolor and collage.
Book design by Erica Weisz
Printed in Malaysia

10 9 8 7 6 5 4 3 2 1
www.trismbooks.com

WRESTLING DREAMS

COLT CABANA
PROFESSIONAL WRESTLER

WITH
SAM + ERICA WEISZ
PROFESSIONAL AUTHORS

ERICA WEISZ
PROFESSIONAL ILLUSTRATOR

Trism Books
Turning Pages. Growing Minds.

"BOOM! BOOM!"
Colt yelled as he jumped
off the top rope.

This was his best ring yet!

Most moms would have scolded,
"Mattresses belong on beds!"
but Colt's mom just shook her head
with a big smile.

She knew their mattresses
always ended up in the
living room.

Colt rode his mattress down the stairs,

squeezed his sister's mattress through the hall,
and flipped his brother's mattress over the railing.

As the collection of mattresses continued to grow,
so did his dreams. . .

During breakfast he dressed in wrestling gear. . .

until his dad performed a maneuver of his own.

Colt used the neighborhood cat, Dusty,
to help with his wrestling entrance...

until his neighbor lectured,

Colt practiced his moves
by hanging on Mrs. Russell's clothesline. . .

On the playground, Colt bench pressed
his friends. . .

By the end of most days,
Colt felt discouraged.

But his mom was always there,
shaking her head with a big smile.

So he banded with friends, Shawn and Marty,
who also believed in their dreams.

They trained on jungle gyms. . .

ate orange vegetables and red protein. . .

and studied their favorite heroes from the crowd.

After all of Colt's hard work,
could his dream come true?

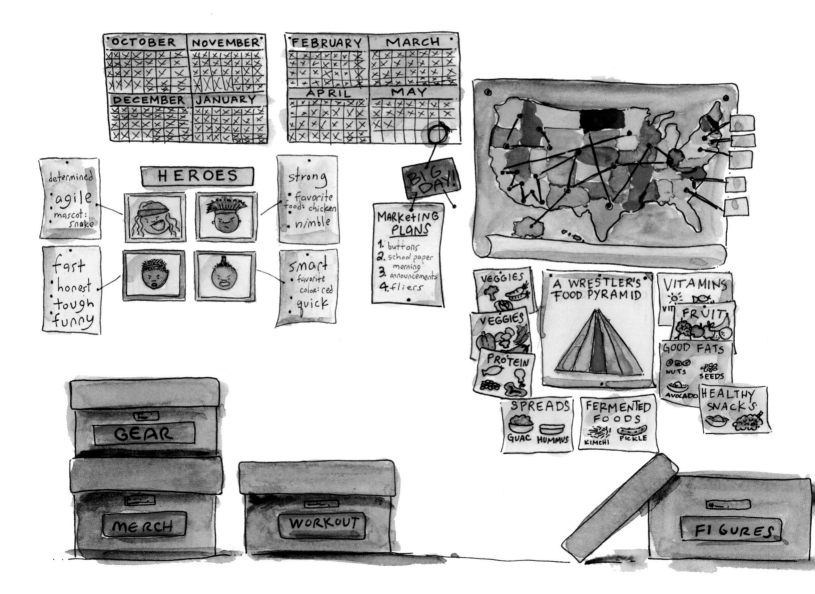

Finally, one recess, he was ready to find out.

IT'S
COLT CA
BA NA!

Everyone came out to watch the exhibition,
even the 6th graders.

He high-fived hands as Shawn and Marty
cheered him on,
"Colt! Colt! Colt!"

As Colt ran down the pavement to the makeshift
ring, his theme song echoed in his ears. . .

His dad's favorite tie wrapped around his head. . .
"Colt! Colt! Colt!"

Dusty followed him into the ring. . .
"Colt! Colt! Colt!"

Colt moved with precision,

jumping off the
ropes,

into the splash,

and dropping the big boot.

As he went for his signature move. . .
"COLT. . . COLT. . ."

The recess supervisor screeched, the neighbor
lectured, and Mrs. Russell scolded.
All shaking their heads, discouraged.

But Colt didn't hear them over
the cheers of his friends.
Marty and Shawn raised Colt's hand in victory.

As Colt's friends carried him off in celebration,
he could see his Mom nodding her head. . .
with a big smile.

A Note from Colt Cabana

As a kid growing up, the only thing I ever
really wanted to do was be a professional wrestler.
I turned everything in my surroundings
into a wrestling scenario. My passion was born!

I hope you feel inspired to live your dream.
Who's in *your* corner?
Look to those people who believe in you,
and believe in yourself.

Always remember to be different,
be unique, and like what you like!